# Mouse Calls

WRITTEN BY
ANNE MARIE PACE

ILLUSTRATED BY
ERIN KRAAN

BEACH LANE BOOKS
NEW YORK   LONDON   TORONTO   SYDNEY   NEW DELHI

Mouse
calls
Moose.

Moose
calls
Goose.

Goose calls Dog

and Hog

and Hare.

Hare calls Bat.

Bat calls Cat.

Cat calls Frog

and then calls Mare.

"Where is Fox?"
Mouse asks Whale.

"Have you seen Ox?"
Mouse asks Snail.

Snail calls
Loon.

Loon calls
Raccoon.

Raccoon
calls Gnu,

then Ewe,

then Bee.

Ewe calls Mink.

Mink
calls Skink.

Skink calls Bug,

"Where is Bee?"
Mouse asks Flea.

"Bee is calling
Chimpanzee."

Chimpanzee
calls
Kangaroo.

Kangaroo
calls
Caribou.

Caribou calls Cockatiel.

Cockatiel calls
Cockatoo.

Cockatoo calls,
"Yoo-hoo, Parrot!"

Parrot answers, "I'm with Ferret."

Mouse
calls Fawn.

Fawn calls Swan.

Swan calls
Clam

and
Ram

and
Lamb.

Lamb calls Grouse,

and Grouse
calls Louse.

Then all the
friends call...

FOR THOSE WHO HELP OTHERS WEATHER ALL OF LIFE'S MANY STORMS—A. M. P.

FOR MY DEAR FRIENDS WHO HAVE ALWAYS BEEN THERE THROUGH THE STORMS, KAILA AND SHERI—E. K.

BEACH LANE BOOKS
An imprint of Simon & Schuster Children's Publishing Division
1230 Avenue of the Americas, New York, New York 10020
Text © 2022 by Anne Marie Pace
Illustration © 2022 by Erin Kraan
Book design by Lauren Rille and Lissi Erwin © 2022 by Simon & Schuster, Inc.
All rights reserved, including the right of reproduction in whole or in part in any form.
BEACH LANE BOOKS and colophon are trademarks of Simon & Schuster, Inc.
For information about special discounts for bulk purchases, please contact Simon & Schuster Special Sales
at 1-866-506-1949 or business@simonandschuster.com.
The Simon & Schuster Speakers Bureau can bring authors to your live event. For more information or to book an event,
contact the Simon & Schuster Speakers Bureau at 1-866-248-3049 or visit our website at www.simonspeakers.com.
The text for this book was hand-lettered by Erin Kraan; additional text was set in Quisas and Belizio.
The illustrations for this book were rendered in woodcut prints and digital collage.
Manufactured in China
0422 SCP
First Edition
10 9 8 7 6 5 4 3 2 1
Library of Congress Cataloging-in-Publication Data
Names: Pace, Anne Marie, author. | Kraan, Erin, illustrator.
Title: Mouse calls / Anne Marie Pace ; illustrated by Erin Kraan.
Description: First edition. | New York : Beach Lane Books, [2022] | Audience: Ages 0–8. | Audience: Grades K–1. |
Summary: Mouse calls Moose to tell him of an impending storm, then Moose calls Goose, Goose calls Dog, and so on
until all of the animals are safe and accounted for.
Identifiers: LCCN 2020055020 (print) | LCCN 2020055021 (ebook) | ISBN 9781534453753 (hardcover) | ISBN
9781534453760 (ebook)
Subjects: CYAC: Stories in rhyme. | Animals—Fiction. | Storms—Fiction.
Classification: LCC PZ8.3.P112 Mou 2022 (print) | LCC PZ8.3.P112 (ebook) | DDC [E]—dc23
LC record available at https://lccn.loc.gov/2020055020
LC ebook record available at https://lccn.loc.gov/2020055021